The Prometheus Incident:

A Martian Murder Mystery

Joseph H.J. Líaigh

To my family; my wife, Mandy, and my sons, Timothy, James and John, who have had the misfortune of putting up with me and have done it graciously and generously.

Published by Leach Publications
PO Box 2123, Parkdale, Vic. 3195, Australia.
Email: leachpublications@gmail.com

First published in Australia 2015
Copyright © Leach Publications 2015
Cover design: pro_ebookcovers
Editor:Anita Saunders

ISBN: 978-0-9943481-1-1

Liaigh, Joseph H.J.
THE PROMETHEUS INCIDENT: A Martian
Murder Mystery

Cover photography courtesy of NASA

Acknowledgments:

This book would not have been written without the encouragement and support of me family. This is particularly true of my brother Anthony, who gave invaluable advice on how to structure and develop the story.

I would also like to thank the members of the Melbourne University Science Fiction Club who provided the first forum for my writing.

Finally, thanks to Julie Postance for her encouragement and technical advice and to Anita Saunders for her kind words and editing skill.

Chapter One – The Discovery

The most surprising thing about the whole affair was that it had been so easy. It had been necessary to turn the computer off, then do a survey range over the landing area until a strong surface reflection was picked up, a reflection that was strong enough to indicate free metal on the surface. After that, there was only the one simple three-second burst with the beam on full power. A burst designed to penetrate rock, a burst that would run along wires, jump circuit breakers, burnt out circuit boards and explode computer chips. There had been no dread, no feeling of death. A green light on the panel had indicated that the job was completed. Then the computer was turned back on and everything proceeded as normal. Memory, however, can be a strange and powerful thing. Sleep didn't come easily. The present was haunted by memory, haunted by a memory of hanging weightless in a cramped, familiar space, facing a battery of electronic controls: a computer quietly monitoring the instrumentation.

The mission commander sat back in the fake leather of the driver's seat and gazed out the front-view port of the MERV (Mars Extended Rover Vehicle). She looked across the red wind-eroded sand to the derelict spacecraft, still standing after all these years. Its white ceramic hull looked pink under the reddish Martian sky and it was partially covered by the fine red dust that seemed to cover everything on Mars. The space-suited figure of her second-in-command emerged from the derelict and waved to her.

"I've finished, skip," he called over the radio, "but it doesn't make sense. I just don't see how this could've happened. Even the suit circuits are blown. Two of them didn't have much time at all. They were outside when it happened and their suits failed. They managed to get back to the ship but, without the electrics, they couldn't operate the airlock. The one inside, DeWitt, he died a long time after the other two. He had time to scribble something on the wall. I'll send the image over to you."

"OK, Bob," she replied.

She looked at the image on the heads-up display, superimposed over the Martian landscape. There, in an untidy scrawl, she read; 'They've got to me. I should have known they would. I was so close. I wish I had time to write the details.'

"Hey, Bob," she called back. "Who do you suppose he was talking about? Who got to him? This was a simple exploration expedition. What's he talking about?"

"Beats me, boss," Bob O'Brian answered. "But whoever they were, they did a good job. There's not a whole circuit anywhere on the ship." He looked about him at the flat red plain extending uninterrupted to the horizon. "I don't know what the hell he thought he was close to. This is the middle of the fucking Hellas Basin. He wasn't close to anything!"

The commander sighed. "OK," she said. "Document as much as you can and download what's left of the computer memory. Maybe someone else can figure it out." She frowned. This was meant to have been a simple historic site survey, but right from the start it had been clear there were things about it that she hadn't been told, that she didn't understand. She turned to the main communications panel and typed in a six-digit code. This gave her direct, secure access to the director of the United Nations Space Agency in Geneva. The access and secrecy that afforded was unheard of in Mars operations, but her message was even more unusual.

"Good morning, sir," she said. "This is Commander Ramasami. The code word is Alpha." She closed the channel, knowing it would take more than twenty minutes for her message to get to the director. She looked around at the red sandy plain that formed the bottom of the Hellas Impact Basin. Code word Alpha meant that the deaths were the result of a complete electronics failure, something that was almost unimaginable. How had he known that these weird circumstances were a possibility? Another mystery. Her frown deepened as she looked at the two long dead figures lying at the foot of the derelict, their spacesuits almost buried in the red dust. There were too many mysteries associated with this mission. She didn't like mysteries. On Mars, mysteries could get you killed.

Chapter Two – The Assignment

It had all been so easy: easy to do, that is; not easy to live with. There was a price to be paid. Those few moments had meant that there was a darkness that constantly reached from the past and discoloured every success, every triumph and every joy. All of life was now haunted and the ghosts who did the haunting were never far away.

Detective Inspector Richardson was just about to begin Sunday dinner with his family, a tradition he tried very hard to hold on to, when the doorbell rang. His heart sank. He couldn't even get this one night alone.

"I'll get it!" Tommy, his youngest, called, running off before anyone could stop him. He came back very subdued. "There are some people there for you, Dad," he said. Richardson sighed. Just once he would like to eat a full Sunday dinner in peace. He walked to the door to find his boss, Chief Inspector William Gordon, waiting there. Behind him were two young uniformed men, both standing stiffly erect. He didn't recognise the uniforms but they weren't just neat, they were immaculate, as if they were about to go on parade.

His boss looked at him apologetically. "Sorry to interrupt your dinner, Frank," he said. "But this is going to be a long one – a lot of pressure from high up, really high up." Richardson was studying the young men behind his boss. They hadn't moved.

Ridiculously neat uniforms and strict discipline; who were these guys? It was then that he noticed the United Nations insignia on their arms. This was both unexpected and unfortunate.

Following the violence and financial chaos of the early twenty-first century, the UN agencies had taken more stringent control over the financial and security affairs of the world. The UN had gone from an unwieldy and largely ignored organisation to an ever-tighter confederation of nations. National governments still existed, but they were so bound by treaties and covenants that they could do nothing outside their borders, and precious little inside them, without UN supervision. Presidents and prime ministers were still elected but the real power lay in the hands of those who ran the UN agencies and that led to a good deal of legal tension. Nothing good could cause UN soldiers to turn up at his home on a Sunday night.

"What's going on, Bill?" he asked. "What's the UN here for? What 'do they want?"

His boss shrugged his shoulders and spread his hands in a gesture of helplessness. "I don't know, Frank," he said. "All I know is that this comes from very high up and that they asked for you by name. As far as I can make out, it's something to do with the space agency. That's it. I don't know anything more. They've deliberately kept me in the dark. I don't like it but there's nothing much I can do about it. Let me tell you something, Frank, you need to be careful. There's something really weird going down. These guys are here to take you on a helicopter ride down to the Avalon Spaceport where you will catch the next sub-orbital shuttle to Schiphol. And get this: from there, you will be helicoptered to Geneva where you will be personally briefed by Dr William Chang, the director of the United Nations Space Agency." Richardson looked at his boss as if he had to be kidding. The young men in uniform didn't react in any way.

"Bill, what … I mean … what the hell are you talking about?" Richardson asked. "Why would the director of the UN Space Agency want to brief me? What would he want to brief me about?"

Gordon just shook his head. "I don't know. It doesn't make sense to me either but there's no point in asking me anything else. You now know as much as I do." The detective's wife came and stood behind him.

The chief inspector gave her an apologetic smile. "Sorry, Kate," he said. "I need him. This one's really big."

"Aren't they all?" she asked sarcastically as she handed Frank his coat. She was a policeman's wife. She was used to interrupted dinners. She gave him a kiss on the cheek.

"Give us a call when you can," she said.

Detective Inspector Richardson stepped back in surprise as he was saluted smartly when he walked out the door. He was escorted to an expensive limousine while CI Gordon got into a small police pool car. Richardson was then driven to the local sporting field where a military helicopter was waiting. It took off as soon as he was on board.

As he was flying out over the western suburbs of Melbourne, he was trying to work the puzzle. Why was he, an everyday local policeman, getting called from his evening meal and rushed into a sub-orbital shuttle to Geneva to get a personal briefing from the director of the United Nations Space Agency? Why was he asked for by name? How did the director of the United Nations Space Agency even know that he existed? No obvious answers presented themselves.

Chapter Three – The Meeting

Memory is a strange and powerful thing. It was impossible, of course, but at various times all three of them had appeared, although mostly it was her. They might be walking down a street or sitting at a cafe. Only momentarily, of course, then it would be seen to be a trick of the light or a chance coincidence in clothing and it was a stranger that was being stared at. Once, indeed, almost spoken to: a jaw-clenching memory. What could be said now that could not have been said all those years ago?

The top-floor office was impressive, the size of the antique wooden desk perhaps even more so. Richardson tried to estimate its worth, but gave up at 'a lot'. One wall of the office was a ceiling-to-floor window out of which Richardson could see the city of Geneva glowing in the late afternoon sun. The Alps lined the distant horizon. The man behind the desk was small, neat and full of energy. Richardson recognised him as Director Chang, head of the United Nations Space Agency and, with the current migration programs in full swing, one of the most powerful men on Earth.

He came around the desk to welcome Richardson warmly. "Inspector Richardson, thank you so much for coming," he said. Richardson smiled thinly. He had not been aware that he had any choice in the matter. "I suppose that this must all seem very strange to you. You must wonder why you're here."

Richardson nodded. "The question had crossed my mind," he said.

Chang waved his assistants out of the room and then typed a short code into his wrist computer. The lights in the office flickered once.

"We are now secure," Chang said. "What I am about to tell you is beyond any sort of secrecy classification. You heard that a survey crew has reached the site of the Prometheus Lander?" Richardson gave a brief nod. "Well, they found that every electrical circuit on the lander had been burnt out. There is no way this could happen naturally or by accident. That crew was murdered." When Richardson remained silent, processing the information, Chang continued. "This is now a murder case and a police matter. We need to find the murderer."

"Why me?" Richardson asked.

"Well, the jurisdiction is a bit uncertain," Chang replied slowly. "But it was an Australian crew and all the possible suspects now live in or near Melbourne, so I thought I'd give it to the Australian police."

"It was a UN ship," Richardson pointed out.

Chang nodded. "As I said, the jurisdiction is a bit uncertain, but I have made the decision that it is an Australian Federal Police case and I would like you to handle it personally."

"You're confident that it was the crew then, no other possibility?" Richardson asked. "I seem to remember that there was talk at the time of Martians or other aliens."

"I'm afraid not," Director Chang said with a wry smile. "Mars is, and always was, as sterile as an asteroid – more sterile than some of them. No, the murderer is one of the crew in the orbiter. You simply need to find out who."

"In that case," Richardson said, "I must ask you, Director, what you were doing when the incident occurred and if you know of any tensions among the crew. As I remember it, you were, in fact, the commander of this mission. Were you not?"

"Yes, I was," Chang replied, "and you'll find that I, along with most of the crew, had neither the means nor the opportunity. At the time of the incident, for example, I was giving a video mission report to Earth. This murder would have been difficult to carry out and there are very few of the crew who could have done it. I can make your task a bit simpler. This could only be done by those who had access to the Mars Microwave Sounder. No one else could possibly commit murder from orbit." Chang noticed Richardson glancing reflexively at the disabled data terminal on his wrist. "I will make sure that you have full access to all the mission data and the inquest transcripts," he said. Then he paused thoughtfully before continuing. "As to tensions among the crew, of course there were some: jealousies, personal dislikes, differences of opinion … all the normal things. This is only what you'd expect. The crew weren't chosen for their compatibility. They were chosen because they were very, very good at what they did. They all had big egos and strong, professional agendas. However, they were also all highly disciplined, goal-driven people and none of these tensions seemed out of the ordinary. There was nothing that I would've thought could lead to murder."

"Motive?" Richardson asked.

Director Chang spread his hands in a gesture of helplessness. "Again, I can't help," he said. "I guess we all benefited to some degree. The lander was stuck on the surface and we had been ordered to stay in support until they could be rescued. It would've been a delay of about six months, but when their radio went silent, we were told to come home. So I guess we all got home early and could get on with our lives. The only one who didn't was poor Sam Carter. He was in charge of the maintenance of the lander and his life was pretty much torn apart by the questioning at the inquest. Everyone else was grateful not to have to spend another six months marking time in Mars orbit. I, for example, went on to train for my next command mission, Frank Steinway started his engineering firm and Lisa Proctor started that consultancy, one that has made her a very rich woman. Even Charlie Freeman wrote that landmark paper on what we now call the Freeman Effect … and so on." The director gave a small smile. "Another six months and it might have been called the Kim effect.

Anyway, we all benefited a bit, but I can't see a motive for murder in any of this. All of these people, all of the crew, including me, were very good at their jobs. Six months might have slowed their careers a bit, but not much – not enough to kill for. I'm sorry, Inspector, I can tell you that the murderer must've been one of the crew but beyond that I can't help you." Richardson looked far from happy but he made no comment. "I gave a very complete testimony to the inquest at the time," the director said, "and that will all be in your data package."

Richardson sighed. "Thank you, Director," he said as he got out of his chair and prepared to leave. All through this conversation, the director's manner hadn't changed. It was professional, apparently open and earnest – but then he was a world-class politician and administrator. He was giving nothing away. As he shook hands, Richardson was thinking that this was a long way to come for a short and rather pointless interview. He was on his way to the door when he stopped and turned around.

"Director, how many people know the exact mode of the crew members' deaths?"

"Very few," the director answered. "On Earth? I had the message given to me via a very secure channel and I have now told you. No one else knows."

"I'd like to keep it that way, if you don't mind," Richardson said.

"Consider it done," the director replied. Richardson smiled as he walked out of the office – perhaps it hadn't been that pointless after all.

Chapter Four – Rule Number One

Yes, there was a price to be paid for murder. This strange, melancholy madness was only part of the price. There was more to pay. There was a further payment that would soon be due. Drifting in memory, its mind kept running in circles. Over and over, it asked the now-familiar question – had it been worth the cost? In twenty years it had been unable to find an answer. A newspaper lay open on the table. The headline read: 'Prometheus Found'.

Detective Inspector Richardson leaned back in his seat and gazed out his window. They were so ridiculously expensive that he very rarely travelled on the sub-orbital shuttles. Now this trip, returning home, was his second in twenty-four hours. It was still so new to him that he found the view out the window distracting. To his north he could see the brown contorted mountains of Southern Turkey, while beneath him lay the yellow sands of the Arabian Peninsula, falling rapidly away as the shuttle climbed. Ahead, the thin blue strip of the Arabian Gulf joined the vast expanse of the Indian Ocean.

His only companion on the off-peak flight was a young space agency pilot whose careful nonchalance proclaimed that he had seen it all before. He was paying more attention to the drink dispenser than the view.

Richardson sighed. It had already been a long day and it wouldn't be over when he landed. Still, it had been interesting and it was certainly an interesting problem that he had been presented with. A cold case murder where the evidence was necessarily circumstantial and where means and opportunity indicated a very small group of suspects but where there was no apparent motive. He knew that without a motive he might get a conviction for negligence but the evidence wouldn't be strong enough for murder.

He glanced at the data terminal on his wrist. The 'Sherlock Holmes' icon (the classic Benedict Cumberbach version, not any of the newer remakes) on the screen was still frowning, which meant that the ferret program he had set running had not come up with anything. He sighed again. In crimes such as this, where one of the victims was an attractive young woman, his experience told him that the most likely motive was sex. He had set his ferret to find evidence in the mission logs and initial commission investigation of romantic trouble or liaisons. The frowning icon meant that it had found nothing. He turned to his companion.

"Excuse me," he said. "Is it true that all sexual liaisons are banned between UN Space Agency crew?"

The young pilot smiled. "Sure is," he said. "First thing they teach you in training. Rule one – no sex. Rule two – see rule one. They say it's dangerous because it interferes with crew cohesion and team work."

"Has it ever happened?" Richardson asked.

The pilot nodded thoughtfully. "Yes," he said. "A couple of times, early on, but it's a really bad idea. Not only is it instant dismissal but the agency has this agreement with its friends, and its friends include virtually all of the aerospace industry. You end up unemployed – permanently. You can also be charged with 'conduct endangering a spacecraft' which is an international criminal offence. They take it real serious." The pilot took another sip from his drink. Richardson could guess the answer to his next question but he had to ask it to be sure.

"Could you do it and get away with it? Not get caught?" he asked.

The pilot shrugged. "On Earth? Maybe, in some out-of-the-way hotel. On board a spacecraft?" He shook his head emphatically. "No way. You know if anyone farts. Anyway, if you're the sort of bloke who can't keep his pants zipped, you don't get on a spacecraft in the first place. Trust me." Richardson nodded and lay back in his seat again. Pity, he thought; sex was always such a good motive. Juries had no trouble understanding it. He glanced at his data link – Sherlock was still frowning.

This was the peak altitude of their sub-orbital trajectory. Out the window he could see the

Himalayas away to the north, showing in high relief even at this altitude, and beyond them the Tibetan plateau and on into China. Below him the southern portion of the Indian sub-continent was covered in early monsoonal cloud.

After lust, the next motive on his list was greed. Who stood to gain? He sent his ferret program looking for the obvious – inheritance, insurance policies, etc. He knew that it wouldn't be that simple but he had to check. Sherlock frowned. Nothing obvious then; still, there were other ways to benefit from a murder: indirect benefit or planned benefit. He went over the briefing he had just been given in his mind. This gave him the germ of an idea. He whispered some instructions to his data link and set his ferret off in a new direction. Almost immediately, the Sherlock icon smiled. He reviewed the collected data and gave some further instructions. He had his interview list fully formed by the time they crossed the West Australian coast and as the shuttle rotated for re-entry, he knew the questions he had to ask and how he had to ask them.

He was met at the Avalon Spaceport by Peter Wilson, his sergeant, in an unmarked police car. Wilson was a pleasant young man: ambitious but patient and eager to learn – a good combination.

"Where to, boss?" he asked cheerfully.

"University of Melbourne," came the reply. "The new Climate Sciences building." Detective Inspector

Richardson climbed into the passenger seat and stared pensively out the window. "No," he said pre-emptively. "I don't need to discuss anything at the moment." Sergeant Wilson knew better than to chat when the boss was thinking. They drove up to Melbourne in silence.

Chapter Five – The Freeman Interview

Professor Freeman sat behind his desk in silent contemplation. He had signed all the necessary papers and read his morning mail. There would be nothing urgent to demand his attention until he met with the academic board at 11.00 a.m. Still, it was not a happy meditation. Professor Freeman gazed out the window in a dark and sullen melancholy. He was an impressive, handsome-looking man in his early fifties. He had a patrician air about him which was enhanced by his prematurely grey hair. This was swept back in a conservative style which matched the classic tailoring of his suit. His desk and office were as neat and orderly as his attire. He was the epitome of the modern, managerial academic. The brooding nature of his contemplation would have surprised his professional colleagues. It seemed to them that he was still riding the academic tide that he had caught twenty years ago: a tide which had brought him some remarkable success. A newspaper lay neatly folded on his desk. Its headline read: 'Hellas Basin expedition locates the Ares II Lander'. His personal assistant knocked on his door and stuck her head into the office. He looked up immediately, glad of the distraction from his dark mood.

"There's a Detective Inspector Richardson from the Australian Federal Police here to see you, Professor," she said. "Okay, send him in," he told her. He then turned and gazed out his tenth-storey window. It was spring and the elm trees that dotted the campus were a vivid green.

As Detective Inspector Richardson walked into the office Professor Freeman turned to face him and motioned for him to sit down. Detective Inspector Richardson was a heavy, thickset man in a cheap and undeniably worn suit. A younger man, slimmer and much better dressed, followed him in but remained standing near the door. Richardson moved with slow, deliberate motions and he had the slightly frayed look of someone who had not slept.

As he sat down he said, "Thank you, Professor. I would like to ask you a few questions, if you don't mind."

"Of course," said Professor Freeman with a casual insincerity. "I'm always ready to help the police in any way I can." He leaned back in his chair and watched the detective closely.
Detective Inspector Richardson spoke slowly and carefully. "As one of the members of the Ares II crew, I'm sure you're aware that the latest mission to the Hellas Basin has found the remains of your lander, the Prometheus, and that a preliminary onsite investigation has been able to determine that the crew died of apoxia."

"Yes, certainly. It has been on my mind all morning. The whole thing is just so sad. They were good people. They were people I was proud to call my friends," Freeman replied, "This news has just brought the whole tragic thing back." He paused and examined Richardson closely. "I am curious though as to why this interests the police department?" Wrong reaction, Richardson thought. He's way too calm. It's almost as if he was expecting us. Why? "Well, Professor," Richardson said, "we have reason to believe that they were murdered ..." Professor Freeman stopped listening as the office seemed to fade into memory, memory of a time spent weightless in the close confines of a spaceship. It was all so long, long ago.

"Professor Freeman?" Freeman became aware of his surroundings with a start. Richardson smiled. "You seemed to be a little lost there."

"I'm sorry," replied Freeman, "but the news you just gave me came as a shock: a real shock. Why do you think they were murdered? Who could have done it?"

"Well, to answer your second question first. Considering the location, it's obvious that the only reasonable suspects are the fifteen people who were the crew of the Ares II., I have been told that there is no natural force that could produce the circumstances of their death, so it seems that foul play is very strongly indicated. In fact, we know that they were murdered. We need to interview all of the crew members to find which of them was responsible. You were the atmospheric physicist on board the mission, correct?"

"Wait. Am I a suspect? Are you accusing me?" Professor Freeman was incredulous and angry. "This is preposterous! Surely it was an accident! How could I have done it? What motive could I have had? What motive could any of us have had?"

Richardson leaned back in his chair and seemed to study the small data terminal on his wrist as he answered. "You know, Professor," he said. "At the moment we're only making general enquiries. These questions are all pretty routine but until we get some clarity, I'm afraid that you and all your crewmates are, indeed, suspects. Motive is, as you say, a puzzle. Normally in a case like this, where you have an isolated group and one of the victims is an attractive young woman, I would consider sex the most likely motive. It's the classic scenario for a crime of passion. However, in this case you were all very highly motivated, ambitious and disciplined people. Also, you had all signed a binding legal contract to refrain from sexual activity for the duration of the mission. I understand that the space agency deals very harshly with crew members who break that agreement – something about it interfering with crew cohesion." Richardson looked to Professor Freeman for confirmation. Freeman nodded.
"In any case, I have been through all of the commander's confidential mission reports and right through the evidence at the original commission of enquiry. There is no indication of any problems in that direction." He looked around the plush office with its large picture windows. "You've done very well for yourself. Being a member of the Ares II crew must've helped a bit."

Professor Freeman frowned. "Look here," he said. "I was on that mission because I'm good at what I do. I got this position because I'm good at what I do. If I hadn't made that trip to Mars, I would still have had a successful career. It may have taken a slightly different route but I would still have gotten to where I am. I didn't need to kill my friends to get here."

Richardson gave an apologetic smile. "Professor, at this stage I'm mostly just collecting background information. What instruments did you use in your atmospheric research?"

Still frowning, Professor Freeman sat back in his oversized leather chair and looked at the detective as he would at a wayward student. "For the most part I used the MaSI, the MOP, and the MMS," he said. Detective Inspector Richardson looked blank. "The Mars Spectrographic Imager, the Mars Optical Polarimeter, and the Mars Microwave Sounder," he clarified.

Once again, the detective seemed to be studying the small data terminal on his wrist. "Did you share any of these instruments with other members of the crew?" he asked. "Was there some sort of roster for their use?'

"I shared the MaSI and the MMS with Dr Martin O'Connor, the geophysicist," the professor replied. "Early on it was very tightly timetabled, but we were well into the extended part of the mission and, truth to tell, had mostly finished our key observations. By that stage, instrument use was mostly sorted by a kind of loose mutual agreement between Martin and myself." The professor looked thoughtful for a moment. "Martin was always a bit strange, brilliant in his own way, of course, but strange. He had a very nice position with a large asteroid mining company all lined up for when he got back, would have set him up for life, but he didn't take it up. When he did actually return, he just wrote a very peculiar book and then ran off and joined some sort of monastery – odd. He was close friends with Colonel Prentice." The detective looked up, suddenly interested. "Nothing untoward," the professor assured him. "Commander Chang made sure of that, but they did spend a lot of time together."

Richardson nodded. "Professor, the Prometheus had suffered an earlier technical problem, had it not?" Richardson asked.

"Yes," Professor Freeman answered. "It had a propulsion failure. It was an ongoing problem with the Boeing Series landers."

"If they had not died in the second incident, this would have delayed your return to Earth, would it not?"

Freeman nodded. "I suppose so," he said.

"Would Dr O'Connor's lucrative asteroid mining job have still been there if your return had been delayed?" Professor Freeman shrugged.

"Probably," he said. "O'Connor was brilliant, although those positions are very competitive."

Richardson stood up. "Thank you for your time and your help, Professor," he said. "We'll interview Dr O'Connor and the other members of the crew in due course. That's all for now but I would appreciate it if you could let us know if you are travelling anywhere in the next few days. I may need to ask a few more questions once I have the whole picture clearer in my mind."

Professor Freeman stood to shake the detective's hand. "Of course," he said. "As I said before, I'm always happy to help the police in any way I can."

Richardson had almost left the room when he turned around. "Oh, one last thing, Professor DeWitt wrote something on the inside of the lander before he died. He wrote: 'They've got to me. I should have known they would. I was so close. I wish I had time to write the details.' Any idea what he meant?"

For the first time, Professor Freeman looked genuinely surprised. "No," he said. "No idea at all."

Chapter Six – Space Jumping

When he got back to the car, Richardson ignored the enquiring look of his sergeant. He tapped the screen on his wrist data terminal and said, "UNSA, I need to get to Mildura ASAP."

"Detective Inspector Richardson, we have a helicopter waiting for you on standby," came the immediate reply. "If you will go to the nearest helipad at the Royal Melbourne Hospital, it will pick you up within half an hour."

His sergeant looked at him in frank disbelief. "Boss, what is going on?" he asked. "What on earth are you involved with?"

"To tell you the truth, I don't think I know half of what is going on," Richardson replied. "And very little of what I know is on Earth. I do know that there has been a multiple murder and I think I know how to catch the murderer. Drive me to the helipad – in a hurry. I'll brief you on the way." Sergeant Wilson shrugged and the car pulled out into the traffic with lights and siren. Less than fifteen minutes later, they were both flying over the northern suburbs of Melbourne on their way to Mildura.

Less than an hour later, Detective Inspector Richardson and Sergeant Wilson walked slowly up the gravel path to a white corrugated iron building with the grandiose title of 'Mildura Space Adventure

Centre' emblazoned in bold, red letters across the entrance. Richardson was still stiff from the two-hour helicopter ride. Military helicopters tended to be built for speed rather than comfort.

A small rocket stood out in the centre of the large concrete pad in front of the building. They hadn't gone far when a siren sounded and red lights around the perimeter of the pad started flashing. Nearby, behind an earthen embankment, there was a shallow concrete trench and wall with a sign that read: 'Shelter here when lights are flashing'.

"Quick, boss, in here," Sergeant Wilson said. They both hurried over and sat down, sheltering behind the wall. A little while later there was a bone-shaking roar as the rocket launched and arced into the sky.

When the sirens were silent and the lights stopped flashing, they got up, watched the path of the rocket for a moment, and then continued on to the building. There was a man waiting for them at the front door. The building was neat but purely functional. The man was neither of those. He was dressed in a shabby and ill-fitting flight suit. His skin had a yellowish cast and he hadn't shaved for some time.

"You looking for a space jump?" he asked. "We've got the latest technology." He looked at Detective Inspector Richardson's figure. "We can handle all body types and haven't lost anyone this month."

Richardson showed his ID. "Detective Inspector Richardson and Detective Sergeant Wilson, Australian Federal Police. We're here to see Samuel Carter."

The man seemed to deflate and his face fell. "You've found him," he said. "Come on in. I've been expecting you."

Inside, most of the building was taken up with two small rockets similar to the one that had just taken off. They were in various stages of preparation, with parts and testing equipment arranged along the side benches. There was a small office at the front and it was here that Samuel Carter and Richardson sat down to talk. Detective Sergeant Wilson remained standing, making careful note of the surroundings.

"You said you've been expecting a visit from the police," Richardson said. "Why is that?"

Samuel Carter gave a resigned shrug of his shoulders and pointed to the newspaper on the desk. The headline, 'Prometheus Found', was in clear, black type. "I figured that you'd know how they died by now and that you'd be coming to pay me a call." Detective Inspector Richardson looked at him quizzically, so he continued. "Given that the original enquiry all but charged me with criminal negligence, I figured that once you had the evidence, you'd be out to complete the job."

"I'm sorry, Mr Carter," the detective said. "But the original enquiry did not have all the pertinent data. Things may have been unfairly implied. We now know that simple negligence was not involved. We have reason to believe that the crew of the Prometheus were murdered."

Carter's first reaction was shock and surprise as he tried to process the information. Then he broke down and started to cry and laugh at the same time. "It wasn't me," he said. "It wasn't my fault. All these years and it wasn't my fault." Richardson waited patiently for him to calm down. Eventually he wiped his tears away with his sleeve and explained. "After the original enquiry, I really thought it was something I'd done or left undone. Along with most of the world, I really thought it was my fault. Now you say they were murdered and that means I had nothing to do with it. All these years and I had nothing to do with it."

"Mr Carter, you were the Ares II crew member responsible for the onboard maintenance of Prometheus and its equipment. Is that true?" Richardson asked. Carter nodded. "Did that include the power systems on the field suits?"

Carter shook his head. "No, they were sealed units," he said. "Wait – is that how they died? Then you're looking for someone who never left the Earth." He paused in thought for a moment and then slammed his fist down on the table. "The Chinese!" he said. "They wanted that mission and those units were manufactured by the Chinese. They must've sabotaged the suit units when they didn't get the mission." Even though he was outraged and angry, his voice still had a slightly puzzled tone, as if he couldn't quite believe his own theory. "But it was our turn. You know? It was Australia's turn."

Richardson consulted his small data recorder. "That's an interesting theory," he said. "Rest assured we will investigate it in due course. Was there any tension among the crew – any jealousies or illicit relationships?"

Carter took a deep breath to calm down and then shook his head firmly. "No," he said. "The commander would have cracked down hard on anything like that. Anyway, I checked that ship and all its gear. At the time I said that I was sure everything was in perfect working order. Now, after all these years, I can say that again. I'm sure all the bits I could check were in perfect working order. Tensions in the crew?" He again shook his head. "Sure, but not relevant. How could any of the crew sabotage the lander? No, it was the Chinese. It must've been."

"Professor Freeman mentioned that Dr O'Connor was close to Colonel Prentice ..."

Carter laughed. "He would, wouldn't he?" he said. "If there was anyone jealous on that ship it was Charlie Freeman. But no, as I said, the commander kept a tight watch and it was all friendly and by the book."

The detective raised an eyebrow. "No, really," Carter insisted. "On a spaceship, there's nowhere to hide. It must've been the Chinese."

Detective Inspector Richardson nodded and then got up from his chair. "Thank you for your time, Mr Carter," he said. "Rest assured, we know they weren't killed by faulty maintenance and we will pursue all possible avenues. One last thing. Professor DeWitt wrote something on the inside of the lander before he died. He wrote: 'They've got to me. I should have known they would. I was so close. I wish I had time to write the details.' Any idea what he meant?"

Carter shook his head. "No. But I wouldn't take much notice of anything DeWitt wrote and nothing he wrote would surprise me." Richardson nodded and turned to go.

As they were leaving, Sergeant Wilson paused at the doorway, looking into the shed. "What is it that you do here?" he asked.

Carter snorted. "They call it space jumping. Rich kids with more money than brains. They take a rocket ride up to 200K and then freefall back into the atmosphere. It seems dangerous but there's an automatic parachute system that gets them down safely. The recovery crew will be bringing in that one you saw take off shortly." He looked around him with something like disgust. "I hate the whole stupid idea but after the enquiry I couldn't get a job anywhere. Let me tell you, I hit rock bottom and stayed there for a long time. This place isn't exactly reputable and it's got bugger all to do with the exploration of space, but it's at least allowed me to crawl my way back."

Richardson nodded. It was a story he had heard many times before, often without the happy ending. He left and they made their way back to the helicopter.

"If he did it, he didn't get much out of it," Wilson commented as they walked back down the path to the helipad.

"I never thought he did it," Richardson replied. "He didn't really have the means, so he wasn't actually on my list of suspects. I just needed some independent background information. You notice that he didn't deny that there were tensions among the crew. He just thought that they weren't relevant. Chang also mentioned tensions. He just didn't think they were anything unusual. We need to find out what those tensions were." He stopped and turned around to look at the ugly prefab building. "I also came to let him know that he was in the clear. What happened to him at the inquest would've been hard to live with. I don't even want to think about the stress he must have been under these last few days."

Chapter Seven – The Monk

It was on the way back to Melbourne that Richardson diverted the helicopter to a deep mountain valley. On the valley floor was a ramshackle collection of buildings centred round a large homestead. This had once been the home of a wealthy pastoralist but now it formed the core of St. Bernard's Monastery. The helicopter set down on the lawn and half an hour later Detective Inspector Richardson was sitting next to a log fire in a stone fireplace, facing a tall, grey-haired monk with piercing blue eyes. Once again, Sergeant Wilson remained standing, leaning against the wood panelled wall.

"Dr O'Connor," Detective Inspector Richardson began, only to be interrupted.

"It's Brother Columba now," the monk told him gently. "I haven't used the other name since I entered the monastery."

The detective nodded, accepting this. "That was not long after you returned from Mars on the Ares II?" he asked. Brother Columba nodded. "You are aware that the Prometheus has been found?"

Brother Columba smiled as he answered. "Yes, the abbot told me this morning after Lauds. Although technically, we always knew where it was, so it hasn't been so much found as visited. Do you have news on how they died?"

"I do, in fact," the detective said. "We believe they were murdered."

Brother Columba was surprised but he wasn't as shocked as the other two. "No," he said. "It may look like it but I don't believe it. Why would anyone do that? It makes no sense. It's far more likely to be some sort of accident."

"We don't think so, Brother," the detective said. "The conditions strongly suggest foul play and we need to interview all the Ares II crew members. One of them is a murderer."

Brother Columba still shook his head. "As I said, it may look like it," he said. "My guess is that Dr DeWitt made some stupid mistake that no safety manual had ever anticipated and caused an accident that just looks weird. Poor old Simon was a brilliant exobiologist but a terrible astronaut. The whole trip, he was just a serious accident waiting to happen," There was a tone of contempt in his voice.

"You didn't like him much, did you?" Richardson asked.

The monk paused and looked into the fireplace. "No, I didn't, God help me," he said, after a short pause. "He was not a very likable man. He thought it was hilarious that Elise and I would take time to pray and he made sure everyone knew it. Mind you, I was far from being on my own in having reason not to like him. Lisa Proctor couldn't stand him. Lisa was too hard-headed, too evidence-based to give his ideas the respect he thought they deserved."

"What ideas were those?" Richardson asked.

"Ideas about the likelihood of finding life on Mars," Brother Columba replied. "Of course, Lisa was right."

"DeWitt wrote something on the inside of the lander before he died," Richardson said. "He wrote: 'They've got to me. I should have known they would. I was so close. I wish I had time to write the details.' Any idea what he meant?"

Brother Columba shook his head. "No," he said. "But I think you can be pretty sure it's fantasy. DeWitt was a sad man in many ways. I think he probably couldn't face the idea he had caused the disaster and convinced himself that it was the work of aliens, trying to keep him from the truth."

"The 'they' in the message could have been the crew of the Ares II," Richardson said. "Perhaps he thought they had all ganged up to murder him."

"Maybe," the monk said with a shrug. "Like I said, fantasy. I really can't see this as a murder. It will have been a weird accident and DeWitt will have been the cause."

The detective consulted his data terminal. "That's the second theory I've been given today," he said. "Samuel Carter thinks it was Chinese sabotage."

The monk smiled. "How is Sam?" he asked. "I'd heard he'd had a hard time of it."

"He seems to be getting things back together," Richardson replied. "Hopefully, this investigation will give him some sort of closure. You don't believe his theory?"

"No," Brother Columba said. "The Chinese certainly wanted the mission. They had this idea that the Hellas Basin would be the best spot for a Mars colony. As it turned out, they were dead wrong but they were certainly annoyed when the Hellas mission went to Australia. Still, the rules said it was Australia's turn, so they couldn't really complain. But if they'd really wanted to stop the mission, there were many far less dramatic ways they could've done it: stopping the funding, for one. No, in the end you'll find it was just a bizarre accident."

"Maybe," the detective said, "but in the meantime I need to ask you some more questions. You were the geophysicist on the mission and your work involved a spectrographic imaging system and a microwave sounder, is that correct?" The monk nodded. "What were you working on at the time?"

"I was doing a spectrographic analysis of some rock outcrops in the Hellas Basin floor, proving to the

Chinese that this was a terrible place for a base," the monk said.

"You weren't using the microwave sounder?" Richardson asked.

Brother Columba shook his head. "No," he said firmly. "We had completed the sounding survey the week before. It would be too dangerous to operate the MMS while there was a ship on the surface."

"You shared that instrument with Professor Freeman. Could he have been using it?"

The monk gave a non-committal shrug. "I guess so," he said. "You could check the instrument logs. It would've been quite safe for him to do the sort of work he did. He used the MMS in a completely different configuration: one with a minimal power output. Charlie's work would've been no threat to anyone on the surface."

"How much power would these instruments use?" Richardson asked. "Would it be possible to monitor the instrument use by looking at the power consumption?"

Brother Columba shook his head. "Not really, their power use was minimal," he said. "The only exception was when we used the MMS for deep crustal soundings. To run it on that power setting, you basically had to shut down the rest of the ship. But we had completed our crustal surveys long before the

Prometheus ever left orbit, so power management was no longer a problem."

Richardson spent a moment looking at his wrist data terminal, verifying the information he had just been given. "I've been told you were good friends with Colonel Prentice," he said. "Is it true that you two had a falling out just before she left for the surface?"

The monk only smiled. "No, and it wasn't the sort of friendship you're suggesting," he said. "The commander would have come down very hard on anything like that. No, it was just that we were both Catholic and we would get together to pray. I had a lot of time to think on the way out to Mars – you have no idea how boring interplanetary travel can be. I was already well on my way to this place while I was still on my way to Mars. I wrote a book about it all when I got back."

The detective nodded and casually consulted his wrist data link. "So I've been told," he said. "Still, I'm sure you can see my concern. A beautiful young woman is murdered and a close friend is not only among the list of suspects but has control of a dangerous microwave instrument. Then, on return to Earth, he gives up his opportunity for a lucrative career to join a monastery. A suspicious person might think that it was not so much a religious calling as guilt – trying to cope with what you had done."

The monk shook his head, still smiling. "You should take up a career in fiction, detective," he said. "No, that story won't wash. First, Will Chang was a very good commander and he was very careful about 'inappropriate' relationships. You need to be in space. He was especially careful with relationships around Elise who was, as you say, very attractive. Secondly, you only have to check the instrument logs to see what I was working on and where. Thirdly, a religious vocation based on guilt would most certainly fail. I would've been out of this place years ago. I'm still sure that it'll turn out to be an accident."

This time the detective shook his head firmly. "No. We know that they were murdered," he said. "There is no natural force or accident that could produce the circumstances of their death."

"Look, I know the circumstances might seem strange," the monk replied. "But I'm still sure it'll turn out to be an accident. You have no idea how far out in left field Simon DeWitt could be."

Detective Inspector Richardson considered the man dressed in black robes. He was used to the guilty making up strange theories to cover their guilt but this man was as cool as an iceberg. He showed no nervousness at all. Richardson didn't know quite what to make of it.

"There is another possible motive we need to explore," he said. "The propulsion failure on the Prometheus would have meant a long delay in your return to Earth. Would the mining company have held your position open that long? Those high-profile positions are very competitive. Perhaps you decided you couldn't risk losing the job, used your microwave thing to destroy the spaceship so that you wouldn't miss the Earth orbit insertion window. Then, on the way back, you have an attack of guilt and decide to punish yourself by coming here." Again the monk smiled broadly – not one of the reactions Richardson was expecting.

"Really, Detective, you should consider a career in fiction," he said. "No, I had already decided not to take that job before the accident occurred. At that stage I didn't know I would be coming here but I did know I wouldn't be going asteroid mining. I'd already let the company know. You can check with them."

Richardson sat looking at the monk in silence for a long time. Then he sighed and stood up. "We will," he said. "Thank you for your time, Brother. Normally, I would ask you to let us know about any travel plans but I guess that's not necessary in your case."

The monk smiled as he shook his head. "No," he said. "I'm not going anywhere."

As they were walking back to the helicopter, Wilson asked, "What do you think about him, boss? Is he on your list of suspects?"

Richardson nodded. "Yes," he said. "He had both opportunity and means. But if that message to the mining company pans out, I just can't make out a motive and my gut is telling me that motive is the key to this case. We know how they were killed, we just don't know why."

"He seemed pretty cool under pressure," Wilson noted. "Your accusations didn't bother him at all."

Richardson frowned. His sergeant was right and that was either very good or very bad. He just didn't know which. "Run those checks on him as fast as you can," he said. "I'd like the results before we get back to Melbourne."

"Sure thing, boss," Wilson said as he climbed into the helicopter.

Chapter Eight – The Consultant

It was just after five o'clock and Dr Lisa Proctor was preparing to leave the office when she was momentarily distracted by the military helicopter that swooped past her window towards the building's landing pad. She wondered briefly who in the building was working on a military contract but quickly went back to preparing the papers she would need for tonight's dinner. It was with a wealthy prospective client and she would need to be ready. Ten minutes later her personal assistant opened her door.

"Lisa, I'm sorry, but there are two men here to see you," he said.

"Not now, Freddie," she said without looking up. "I'm getting ready to go."

"I'm afraid it will have to be now," said a voice she didn't know. She looked up and saw a tired-looking, overweight man in a cheap suit. He held up identification. "Detective Inspector Richardson, Australian Federal Police," he said. He indicated a young, athletic man behind him. "This is my associate, Detective Sergeant Wilson. We are investigating the deaths on the Prometheus. You have read the papers?"

Lisa sighed and turned away to gaze out her window. "Yes," she said. "It brings back memories I'd rather leave buried." Then she turned back to look at Richardson with a puzzled expression on her face. "Why are the police involved?" she asked. "Isn't this a matter for the technical investigation team?"

"Their preliminary investigation has indicated that the crew were murdered," Richardson replied. "We need to understand how and why – and by whom."

Lisa's face went stone still and then turned white. Her grip tightened on the stylus she was holding until it snapped. "It was DeWitt, wasn't it?" she spat. "I knew that idiot was mad. Everyone knew that Mars was as sterile as a hospital autoclave but he had this insane idea that he could find life in the Hellas Basin. A new sort of life based on RNA rather than DNA. It was like a religious quest for him. He would laugh at Elise and Martin, but he was the one who behaved like some weird religious fanatic. He hated the fact that no one else believed the way he did."

"That seems a rather unlikely motive for a murder/ suicide," Richardson commented. "Killed because they didn't believe in Martians."

"You didn't know him," she replied. "He really was a fanatic. If he thought the others were hindering his great work, I can easily believe he would've killed them." She paused thoughtfully. "Don't believe he'd intend suicide though. I think maybe he just killed the two of them and only then realised he didn't know how to work the ship. Stupid bastard."

"You didn't like him?" Richardson suggested.

"No one did," she replied. "The other two were sweethearts, everyone loved them, but he was a bastard. He accused me of faking instrument results just because they didn't match his theory. He should never have been allowed anywhere near a spaceship." She paused and looked thoughtfully at the policemen. "If you think it was murder, then there's something strange about the deaths," she said slowly. "That's why there's so little technical information available. Look, if it's something that would make people believe they were attacked by aliens, then it's definitely DeWitt. He would happily commit suicide if it would convince the world that alien life really was out there. For him, it would be a small lie to serve a greater truth. As I said, the man was a fanatic." Richardson nodded thoughtfully and consulted the data recorder on his wrist. The woman was not just smart but shrewd. She would be good at business – and at hiding a crime.

"DeWitt wrote something on the inside of the lander before he died," he said. "He wrote: 'They've got to me. I should have known they would. I was so close. I wish I had time to write the details.' Any idea what he meant?"

Dr Proctor snorted contemptuously. "That's it. He's trying to get people to believe in these bloody aliens.

Trying to make himself famous by pretending that he was close to proving they existed. What a load of rubbish. Inspector, do you know the story of the mathematician in the early years of the twentieth century who, whenever he set sail across the Atlantic, would send a telegram saying, 'Solved Thermat's last theorem. Details later.' So that if the boat sank, he would go down in history as having solved the theorem? This is the same thing. Look, I died. Ooh, aliens killed me. Pathetic."

Richardson nodded. "Maybe," he said noncommittally. "You were the engineer in charge of the instrumentation on board the Ares II orbiter, correct?" Richardson asked. She nodded. "You had access to all the instruments?" She nodded again. "How much did you dislike Dr DeWitt?"

She frowned. "Not enough to kill him, if that's what you're suggesting. Certainly not enough to kill the other two just to get at him."

Richardson again looked at the small data terminal on his wrist. "In your position, were you in charge of instrument scheduling?" he asked.

Lisa nodded. "Early on," she said. "But we were well past our primary mission by the time the Prometheus incident occurred. By then the scientists mostly worked out the schedule informally among themselves. There were safety protocols, of course. I checked all of those. Why are you interested in the orbital instruments?"

Richardson ignored her question. "I understand all instrument use was logged. Could those logs be tampered with?" he asked.

Lisa shook her head. "No," she said. "They could be turned off but once logged they were secure."

"Were they often turned off?" Richardson asked.

"Only occasionally," Lisa replied. "When the scientist was chasing some crazy private theory of their own, maybe using the instrument in a weird way, and didn't want anyone else knowing what they were up to."

"How much power did these instruments use?" Richardson asked.

Proctor shrugged. "It varied," she said. "In terms of the ship-wide power usage it was mostly trivial. The MMS could be a bit of a power hog on some settings. If you wanted to use it on high power, you had to schedule it very carefully or you could interfere with the normal ship operations. That's why all the high-power stuff had been scheduled for early in the mission." Detective Inspector Richardson sat and looked thoughtfully out the window for a moment; at this level the view was spectacular. Then he stood up abruptly.

"Thank you for your time, Dr Proctor. You have been most helpful," he said. "I will leave you to enjoy your evening. I would ask that you let us know if you plan to leave on any extended travel. We may need to ask further questions." He paused. "Also," he continued, "I would prefer it if you didn't discuss this with any of your former crewmates."

"No problem," she said. "I never see any of them anyway."

Back in the helicopter, during the brief flight back to their car, Wilson asked, "Do you think it's her, boss?"

"Well," Richardson replied, "she had means and opportunity and she clearly had some personal grudge against DeWitt."

"Could it be DeWitt, like she said?" Wilson asked.

Richardson shook his head. "No, not the way they died," he said. He gave a small tired smile. "We have been collecting some strange theories today but hers is the least likely of the lot."

Wilson smiled. "Just as well," he said. "It would've made the arrest very difficult. What's so important about the amount of power the instruments use?"

"There was a power outage on the Ares II right before they lost contact with the Prometheus," Richardson explained. "Vince Lombardi, the ship's chief engineer, reported it to the commission of enquiry but they were so convinced that the problem was Carter that they didn't take much notice of it. It was serious though. He claimed that he had to reboot several crucial systems but he could find nothing wrong, nothing that would cause the outage. He couldn't explain it. I think the commission should've investigated that more closely."

"So, are we going to talk to this Lombardi next?" Wilson asked.

Richardson gave a sad little smile. "It would be hard," he said. "He died on an expedition to Venus seven years ago. Nothing suspicious about the death," he said, forestalling Wilson's question. "His ship took a direct hit from a massive solar flare."

"And that killed him?" Wilson asked.

"He got over a thousand times the safe annual radiation dose in the first ten minutes, so, yes, it killed him," Richardson replied. "Come on, let's get back to the car. I need to get home."

Chapter Nine – More Questions

Richardson walked into the familiar hallway and hung up his coat. The dog ran up to greet him. He consciously shook himself and allowed the case to fall away from his mind. It was still early on and he knew that the best way to make progress was to relax and let his subconscious do the work.

The dog was followed by the kids, with Kate standing at the back smiling, still dressed in her work clothes. She came up and kissed him on the cheek and he put his arms around her and held her tight. Even after all these years, this was all he needed. Holding Kate, he could cope with the remnants of a hard day.

"So, what's this mysterious case about?" she asked when he let her go.

He shook his head. "Can't talk about it," he said. "I don't want to anyway. Tonight, I just want to leave it alone and relax."

"Fair enough," she said. "Come on, your dinner's ready. We've already eaten." He ate his dinner watching the news. The Prometheus story had already been forgotten and no new information was available. For this he was grateful. Information was his only weapon. He knew how the crew of the Prometheus had died and, if he was ever to find the murderer, it was crucial that this remain his secret.

It had been a long time between sleeps, so he went to bed early, even before the kids, and was deeply asleep as soon as his head hit the pillow. He slept well that night, with no dreams that he could remember, and when he woke in the morning, his plan for that day was already set in his mind. There were questions he needed to ask.

Richardson had forgotten that he had asked Wilson to call around early, so he arrived in the middle of the early morning chaos. Richardson had to gulp down the last of his coffee and grabbed some toast to go as he went out to the car, leaving his wife to get the kids to school. She was a patient woman but he knew he would have some making up to do when the case was over.

"Where to, boss?" Wilson asked as he climbed into the car. "You need to go back to the monastery again?"

Richardson shook his head. "No. No more helicopters," he said. He smiled at the fleeting look of disappointment that crossed Wilson's face – rides in high-speed military helicopters were a rare privilege. "Maybe tomorrow. Today, I think I can get the answers I need in Melbourne. I need to go back to the university."

"You want to talk to the professor again?" Wilson asked as he pulled away from the kerb.

"Yes," Richardson answered. "I need to get another opinion about this DeWitt character and his relationship to the rest of the crew."

"You want to call ahead and make an appointment?" Wilson asked.

Richardson sat back and considered for a moment. "No, he said at last. "Let's surprise him. I don't want him to have time to rehearse his reactions." He was a keen student of body language. He knew it often revealed more than the spoken words, but only if it was spontaneous and Professor Freeman didn't strike him as a spontaneous kind of guy.

He walked into the professor's office just barely behind the flustered personal assistant who was trying to announce his arrival. He knew he was being rude but he wanted to upset the professional calm with which he had been met the day before. Once again, however, it was almost as if the professor was expecting them. His only reaction was a slightly raised eyebrow at the abruptness of their entry.

"Once again, welcome, gentlemen," he said. He gestured to the chairs in front of his desk. "Please, be seated. How may I be of assistance?"

"Thank you, Professor," Richardson said as he sat down. "If you don't mind, we need to get an independent opinion on some theories we've been given about what happened to the Prometheus."

Professor Freeman smiled and spread his hands in a gesture of acceptance. "As I said before, I'm always happy to help the police in any way I can."

"Good," Richardson said. "Mr Carter suggested to us that it might have been caused by Chinese sabotage but Dr O'Connor dismissed that suggestion without even giving it much thought."

Professor Freeman nodded. "Martin's right," he said. "I guess it would be possible, they were certainly upset at not getting the mission, but it was a bureaucratic tussle – not something you would kill over. Anyway, what would they gain by sabotaging the mission after it had been allocated? They'd already been assigned the next mission, to the Vastis Borealis."

Richardson nodded. He was disappointed. The professor showed the same cool, detached front that he had encountered yesterday. He was carefully managing any signals his posture might give. "Both Dr O'Connor and Dr Proctor mentioned Dr DeWitt," Richardson said. "Dr O'Connor thought he might have been the cause of some bizarre accident while Dr Proctor suggested that he might have killed the other two crew members for not believing his theories about Martian life. Am I correct in thinking that Dr DeWitt was not well liked aboard the Ares II?"

Professor Freeman nodded. "I don't want to speak ill of the dead," he said, "but he was not a likeable man. He and Lisa really didn't get on. He tried to bully her into accepting his belief in extra-terrestrial life and trying to bully Lisa was never a good option. She was very prepared to hit back – hard. It was all verbal, of course, but there was real tension and most of the crew were on Lisa's side. The commander had to keep a very close watch that it didn't get out of hand."

"Perhaps it did," Richardson suggested. "Perhaps it drove DeWitt to kill or even cause him to be killed himself. Perhaps Dr Proctor hit back: not just hard, but permanently."

Freeman shook his head. "No, I don't believe it," he said. "Look, on any mission like that the crew are going to be a group of ambitious people: all with their own goals, all from different backgrounds. Of course you're going to get the occasional conflict and, in the close confines of a spaceship, these can get very intense. However, you do not get selected onto the crew if you can't cope with conflict. Anyway, as I said, the commander was aware of it and kept a close watch."

"So you don't believe either of these theories?" Richardson asked.

Freeman shrugged carelessly. "They're both possible, I guess, but to me, neither of them seem very probable."

"Thank you, Professor," Richardson said. "I'm inclined to agree with you. There's one more thing, if you don't mind?"

Again Freeman shrugged. "Fire away, Detective," he said.

"Close to the time of the incident, your data recordings were turned off. Why was that?" Freeman looked embarrassed and turned to look out the window before answering. When he turned back he had a rueful grin on his face.

"I was using the polarimeter to image the surface," he said. "Most of my colleagues, then and now, would say that it wasn't only a waste of instrument time but a stupid waste of time. That's why I didn't want it recorded. I was trying to find the kind of light polarisation caused by organic matter. If it had worked it would have been a real coup. I would've been the one to find life on Mars and beaten DeWitt at his own game. It didn't work, of course. Mars is barren. Life just never evolved there."

Richardson stood up. "Well, once again, thank you, Professor. You have been very helpful," he said. It was only momentary, but Richardson noticed a slight relaxation of Freeman's shoulders as they shook hands. Freeman was secretly relived that the interview was over.

Chapter Ten – Tension

"Where to now, boss?" Wilson asked as they got back in the car.

"Downtown," Richardson replied. "We need to talk to Lisa Proctor again."

When they got to Dr Proctor's office, the view from the window was just as spectacular in the morning as it had been the night before. Detective Inspector Richardson couldn't help wondering how anyone got any work done with such a view to look at. He gave a mental shrug and dismissed the idea. It was not his problem. He turned to consider the woman before him. She was handsome rather than beautiful, dressed in an expensive-looking business suit and clearly impatient with this interruption to her day.

"Once again, thank you for agreeing to see us, Dr Proctor," he said.

She gave a rather grim smile. "I don't believe I was given much of a choice," she said.

Richardson ignored the comment. "We have been following up on your comments about Dr DeWitt," he said. "It seems that he was not a well-loved member of the crew. Dr O'Connor, in particular, seems to have had cause to dislike him."

Proctor nodded. "He did," she said. "But it didn't really seem to affect Martin, or Elise either, for that matter. His comments were like water off a duck's back. Martin certainly didn't like him but he also had absolutely no respect for him or his ideas. He thought they were just wild, baseless speculation. So he just didn't care what he said. You know, it was like the chattering from the peanut gallery. He just took no notice. I think it really annoyed DeWitt that he couldn't get under Martin's skin."

"He could get under your skin though," Richardson suggested.

Proctor gave a rueful smile and nodded. "Yes, he got to me," she said. "I hated him but I didn't kill him. I certainly didn't kill the other two. I loved Elise, everyone did, and Bob Cole was one of the noblest and bravest men you could meet." She stood up quickly and turned to look out the window. There was a break in her voice as she said, "I was proud to call both of them friends."

Richardson waited until she composed herself and turned around. "What about Professor Freeman?" he asked. "What was his relationship with DeWitt?"

Lisa Proctor looked a bit vague as she answered. "It was okay, I guess," she said. "I wouldn't say they were bosom buddies but Charlie was one of the few crew members who didn't have an active animosity to DeWitt. I don't think they had much to do with each other."

Richardson nodded and again consulted his wrist data device. "I have a couple of technical questions too," he said. "Who had access to the instruments? Was it the whole crew or only certain crew members?"

"Only the crew members who had a direct need for a particular instrument had access to it," she replied. "Access was password controlled."

"Who administered those passwords?" Richardson asked.

"I did," she replied. "I was responsible for the operation of the whole instrument suite."

"So, by controlling the passwords, you had effective access to all the instruments?" he asked.

"I did anyway," she said. "I had to. I needed to do maintenance and calibration testing."

"And once you had access, was there any restriction on the instruments operation? Was instrument use logged separately?" Richardson asked.

She shook her head. "No, but your data log recorded how and when you had used each instrument," she said. "There was no need for a separate instrument log. You must remember, this was a deep space exploration ship. Everything was limited. There was no room for useless duplication or for frivolous use of the ship's systems." Detective Sergeant Wilson let out an involuntary grunt of agreement. He could not imagine Lisa Proctor being frivolous.

"One last question, if I may," Richardson said. "How secure were the passwords? Were they actually private or were they the sort of 'secret' password that everyone knew?"

"They were secure," she answered. "Not only was I in charge of security but all the orbital survey team members were paranoid that someone else would get to analyse their data before they could. This was their big chance to make their mark scientifically and that was a strong incentive not to share."

Richardson got out of his chair. "Thank you, Dr Proctor," Richardson said as he rose to leave. "We won't take up any more of your time." They shook hands.

"Glad to help," Lisa Proctor said in a voice that suggested the direct opposite.

"Where to next, boss?" Wilson asked as they were going down in the elevator.

"Back to the station," Richardson replied. "I have some reading to do."

Chapter Eleven – Speculation

It took Detective Sergeant Wilson nearly all afternoon to set up the situation room with the sort of security that Richardson had requested. This was actually surprisingly quick. This level of security was most unusual in a police station and would normally have been very difficult to organise. He found, however, that when he mentioned the case he was working on, red tape just seemed to vanish and there seemed to be no limit on the resources available to him. It was clear that someone with a lot of influence wanted this case solved and fast. The priority that this gave his requests pleased Wilson even as it made Richardson, who had spent all afternoon in his office reading, very nervous. Richardson inspected the room quickly but carefully when he walked in in the late afternoon.

He simply said, "Good, this'll do nicely," as he sat in one of the armchairs provided.

"I ran a probability matrix on the Forensic AI Engine," Wilson said. "It rated O'Connor and Proctor as the most likely, although all of them had a pretty low probability score."

"And yet someone did it," Richardson said dismissively. "Trust AI to tell you the bleeding obvious."

Wilson looked at his boss. Richardson had a habitual 'shabby' look about him but Wilson knew that he was much smarter than he let on. Most people who looked at him simply thought he was old for his rank and disregarded him as a journeyman police constable who had probably been promoted one step too many. Wilson, however, knew that Richardson had turned down several major offers of promotion. He hadn't asked why but he suspected that it was simply because he disliked meetings and forms: he would rather be a policeman than an administrator. He was conservative, certainly. A product of that generation that reacted to the wild excesses of the early twenty-first century. But that didn't mean that his mind was slow, or ridged, or closed. Wilson came from another generation, one open to new ways of doing things but that didn't mean that he underestimated his boss. He sat down next to Richardson.

"How was your reading, boss?" he asked.

"Interesting," Richardson replied. "I read O'Connor's book, the one Freeman described as strange. It's a kind of spiritual memoir of a journey on a spaceship. As the trip proceeds, O'Connor becomes increasingly disenchanted with planetary science, not because he doesn't believe in it or find it interesting but because he finds it too easy. He wants to stretch himself, to do something much harder."

"By becoming a monk and praying all day?" Wilson asked, incredulous.

Richardson nodded. "Basically, yes," he said. "At least that's the way the book's written. Anyway, while he was mostly focused on his own inner journey, the book contains a lot of insights into the crew dynamics on board that ship. That was a very valuable couple of hours. Now, let's get started."

"Okay, boss," Wilson said. "I thought we'd start with the basics." One wall dissolved into a series of holographic images of a spaceship partially buried in the red dust of Mars. These were followed by images of the three bodies: two outside in spacesuits and one lying on a bunk inside the ship. "This is the crime scene," Wilson continued. "We obviously don't have access to it so we need to rely on the report of the technical team – only we don't have that either. All we have …"

"Is a personal briefing given to me by the head of the UN Space Agency," Richardson finished. "The crucial part of which, the part which has been kept an extraordinarily well-guarded secret, was that they died because all their electrical circuits were burnt out by a massive induced current and that the only thing that could have done that was a full power burst from the Mars Microwave Sounder instrument. Okay, let's push on."

"Right," Wilson said. "We only have four suspects: Carter, Freeman, O'Connor and Proctor." Their images appeared on the wall. "The others were either the alternate surface crew, who were confirmed asleep at the time, or those crew members concerned with the maintenance and navigation of the Ares II itself. None of them had access to the sounder instrument."

"You can get rid of Carter too," Richardson said. "He didn't have access to the MMS and the damage to the ship was well beyond anything he could reasonably be expected to carry out by way of sabotage." Wilson nodded and Carter's image disappeared from the wall.

"We have these three then," Wilson continued. "All three had access to that sounder thing, so they all had the means. Freeman and Proctor also had opportunity: there's no record of what they were doing at the time in question. O'Connor seems to alibi out here. The data recording systems show him using that other thing, the imaging gizmo, right through this time period."

"Leave him in anyway," Richardson said. "The guy was a scientific genius and he knew these systems really well. I'm not sure we can trust the integrity of those data recordings." Wilson nodded and O'Connor's image stayed on the wall.

"That brings us to motive," Wilson said. "Two of these have obvious motives. O'Connor had a very lucrative job offer which would have been placed in jeopardy if the Prometheus crew had lived. I checked his communications log. He was certainly expressing doubts about taking the job but he didn't finally turn it down until after the incident."

"He lied to us?" Richardson asked. Wilson looked doubtful.

"Maybe," he said. "It's also possible he just didn't remember properly. How precise is your memory after twenty years? As I said, he was expressing doubts about the job much earlier. You read his book. What do you think?"

Richardson spoke slowly and thoughtfully. "I think he would be capable of killing," he said. "But not for money or career; certainly not for something as mundane as a job opportunity. He's driven by other motivations."

"What about the conflict with DeWitt?" Wilson asked. "He said DeWitt would laugh at them for praying."

"But in a fairly matter-of-fact sort of way," Richardson said. "There was no real bitterness. If anything, there was a sort of regret that he couldn't bring himself to like DeWitt. He also mentions this in the book but again, only in passing. I think Proctor is right. I don't think DeWitt bothered him. He may be a monk now, but there was a great deal of intellectual arrogance in the man who wrote that book. I think he mostly just ignored DeWitt as an unimportant nuisance."

"Well, that brings us neatly to Proctor," Wilson said. "She really hated DeWitt – maybe enough to kill him. The thought of spending another six months with him, in the close confines of a spaceship, may have just been too much."

Richardson shook his head. "No, I don't think so," he said. "I don't think her antagonism to DeWitt could possibly be bad enough to cause her to kill two innocent crewmates just to get at him."

"Well, he bullied her, humiliated her and accused her of falsifying data," Wilson pointed out. "That may have pushed her to the point where she regarded the others as just unfortunate collateral damage. To me, she seemed a bit too sorry about the death of the other two. That may have been guilt playing itself out."

"Maybe," Richardson said, "but I doubt it. Let's keep going."

"Well, there's the business of the message DeWitt scrawled on the wall of the lander," Wilson said. "Who did he think had gotten to him and what was he close to?"

Richardson shook his head. "No, he said. "Even if it's not just dying ravings and has some connection to reality, which I'm inclined to doubt, it's too vague to be of any use. I'm ignoring that as fantasy. Let's move on."

"Well, that brings us to Freeman," Wilson said, "and his motive is the weakest of the lot. Sure, he's had a stellar academic career but …"

"But he was almost as bright as O'Connor and would have had a great career anyway," Richardson continued. "Damn! My gut is telling me that motive is the key to this case but there's nothing here that works. Let's try a different angle. Do you notice anything about all the theories we were given?"

"They were all wrong?" Wilson suggested.

Richardson gave a wry smile. "Yes, Sergeant," he said. "They were all wrong but they were all wrong in a very particular way. All of our suspects are highly intelligent but in one respect they have all shown a remarkable lack of imagination. All of them suggested a problem that occurred on the surface of Mars. Carter suggested an equipment failure caused by sabotage: an equipment failure that occurred on the surface. O'Connor suggested a weird accident caused by DeWitt's incompetence – on the surface. Proctor suggested that DeWitt killed his crewmates – on the surface. The Prometheus' crew died on the surface so they all assume the cause must be something that happened on the surface. None of them considered that the killing could've been done from orbit, even though they all knew about the MMS."

Wilson shrugged. "They could be lying," he said. "You know, making up some weird story to throw us off the track."

"That could be true of the killer, but unless you're suggesting all three were in it together, two of these people are innocent," Richardson pointed out.

"Yeah, well, maybe they just didn't think of it," Wilson suggested. "You know, like those puzzles where the answer is obvious once you know it but you need to sort of step out of your normal way of thinking to get to it. Maybe to them, this MMS was just a scientific instrument and they didn't see it any other way. It was just natural for them to think that if people died on the surface, then whatever killed them must have happened on the surface."

Richardson sat back in the chair and stared intently at the three images on the wall. "That's not true of one of these," he said slowly. "One of these knew." He was speaking slowly but his mind was racing. He knew the answer.

"Yeah, boss," Wilson said. "But the question is: which one?"

"No," Richardson replied firmly. "The question is why and how can we prove it? Motive is the key. Without a decent motive we have no hope of a conviction."

"There's another possibility, boss," Wilson said. Commander Chang's face appeared on the wall. "He was the commander of the ship and all those mission reports, those reports that played such an important part of the original inquest, the reports that we have been relying on; well, he wrote them. He could easily have misled everybody."

"How could he do it?" Richardson asked. "He didn't have access to the MMS."

"He was the commander of the whole thing!" Wilson said. "I'll bet he had some command override code or something that let him have access to any system on that ship. Look, at the time of the accident, Freeman was using that polarimeter thing, whatever that is, and O'Connor was using the imaging thingy. No one was using the MMS."

"So they say. We only have their word," Richardson pointed out.

"Yes, but it means that it's possible that Chang took control of the MMS without anyone else knowing about it," Wilson insisted.

"Okay," Richardson said. "What's his motive? Sure, he's now rich and powerful but that would have happened anyway. He was renowned for his driven ambition. There's no strong connection with the delay coming back from Mars."

"Sex," Wilson said. "You remember what O'Connor said? That Chang was very protective of Colonel Prentice. What if that was more than just the care of a commander? What if he made an advance and she rejected him? Rejected, scorned. Lust is a great motive for murder and he could easily keep that out of the mission logs that he himself was writing."

"Maybe," Richardson said doubtfully. "But I don't really buy it. He was known to be ambitious and he would have been risking an awful lot for a tumble in the airlock."

"Perhaps they had already had an affair and she threatened to expose him," Wilson suggested.

"Then why start this investigation?" Richardson asked. "Why not just use your influence to downplay the evidence and let it fade into history as a great unsolved mystery? Why not let DeWitt's fellow travellers develop great conspiracy theories about alien invasions and the UN's attempt to hide them? He'd be off scot free."

"Do you want me to take him off the board then?" Wilson asked.

Richardson was silent for a long time. Eventually he said, "No. Leave him up there and bring back the first image, the one of the ship." The image of the ship returned to the wall. Richardson stared at it intently.

"Why?" he asked. "Not just why were they killed, but why was this investigation given to me? This is way out of my normal experience."

"Hey, don't short-change yourself, boss," Wilson said. "We're also good at what we do."

"Yes, we are," Richardson agreed. "But what we do isn't this. As far as the UN is concerned, we're provincial policemen with a purely local jurisdiction. Why wasn't this given to a UN investigative team with a whole bunch of high-powered investigators and lawyers?"

Wilson shrugged. "Keeping a low profile maybe," he suggested. "They may not want a lot of publicity. Also, while the incident occurred on Mars, it was an Australian crew aboard an Australian ship, so we certainly have some claim at jurisdiction."

"Maybe," Richardson agreed. "But it was technically a UN ship and something here just doesn't smell right."

Chapter Twelve – A Proposal

On the floor of the Hellas Basin, Mars, Bob O'Brian walked onto the control deck of the MERV. He walked straight over to the main control screen and typed in a code known only to himself – all electrical power to the control deck died.

Ravi looked at him surprised, "Bob, what did you do?" she asked.

"Sorry, skip," he answered. "No power means no recording. We have five minutes before the safety overrides turn the power back on. Look, we've finished up outside and the bodies are all packed away. We're ready to go, but I thought that you might need to see this. It's Colonel Prentice's field notebook." Ravi took the battered notebook: graphite pencil and paper, an old technology, one not prone to failure. She looked at a list of traverse directions, sample locations and comments. "Read the last page, skip," Bob said.

Ravi flipped through to the last entry. She read it and looked at her second-in-command in astonishment. Then she relaxed. The worried frown disappeared from her face. This explained many of the mysteries that swirled around this trip and she could see why Bob didn't want this recorded without consulting her first. The note had been written as the colonel was dying and it was outstanding in its warmth, pathos and humanity. It was also political dynamite.

"Bob, could you pass me that security envelope that you are conveniently holding in your hand?" He smiled as he handed it over. She put the notebook in the envelope and wrote: 'Most Secret. Director's Eyes Only. Strict Liability Applies.' She showed the address to her second-in-command. "Do you agree?" she asked.

He nodded. "Good move, skip, on all sorts of levels," he said. She sealed the envelope. Then she looked out at the red sandy plain extending to the horizon. It was a hard and empty place. The contents of the note played on her mind, feeding into ideas that she had been playing with for a while now. She looked across at Bob O'Brian. He was a bit taller than her, with ice-blue eyes and a face that seemed to be constantly on the verge of a smile. He had been her 2IC for three years now and she was very fond of him. She also knew he had turned down a number of good promotion opportunities to stay with her, so she figured that he must be fond of her too. In fact, it had been three years of secretly longing for things only spoken of in silent looks and laconic asides. He was a good man but not ambitious: a strong supporter rather than a leader. If she waited for him, she might be waiting until it was too late.

"You know, Bob," she said casually. "I'm thinking of leaving the service. What do you know about the old Polish base on the South Argyre rim?"

"Fairly shallow permafrost and good deep oxide deposits at the base of the scarp. Some nice equipment too," he said. "Almost ideal from a resource point of view. The Poles only left it because of the financial crisis in 2070. Why do you ask?"

"It's just been listed as abandoned and open for salvage," she replied. "It would make a great homesteading opportunity. Of course, I would need someone to help with running the place."

Bob O'Brian watched her with his habitual sly smile playing at the corners of his mouth. "Skip, exactly what are you suggesting?" he asked.

"I'm 32, Bob," she replied. "I've still got some time but the clock is ticking. Father Mulcahey will be at Schiparelli Base for the funerals when we get back. We could ask him to perform another service. What do you think?"

"I think it's taken you long enough to ask and that the colour of this uniform never really suited me," he replied smiling. "I also think I'm going to have to load Polish into my translator app or I'm never going to be able to get that gear up and running again."

She smiled; his reply was so typical of him. "What you really need to do is buy a ring," she said.

Chapter Thirteen – Accusation

That night Richardson lay in his bed, staring at the ceiling and listening to his wife's soft breathing. He was exhausted but his mind wouldn't sleep. He kept going over the case in his head. He was pretty sure that he knew who the murderer was but he just couldn't see a convincing motive. It was while he was reviewing the data for perhaps the twentieth time that he remembered a chance comment by the space agency director and another comment by Lisa Proctor. He put the two together and thought about the crew and their motivation for going on the mission in the first place. They weren't all driven by a thirst for adventure, or for money, or for popular fame. Some were driven by altogether more austere and obscure motives and not all of those ended up in a monastery. This formed the germ of an idea, one he could test.

He carefully got out of bed and whispered some instructions to his data link, careful not to wake his wife. Sherlock smiled almost immediately. He reviewed the data: publication dates and citations. It all fitted. He lay back in bed and now drifted easily towards sleep. He knew what he had to do tomorrow. One small doubt nagged in his mind: this was such a small motive for such a large crime. Also, it was too easy. He gave a mental shrug, he had seen people killed for far less and sometimes you just got lucky.

The next morning, Professor Freeman looked at the untidy detective in front of him, and his offsider standing casually by the door, with barely concealed contempt. He used all his twenty years of experience on university and government committees to control his impatience and dislike.

"While I like to be cooperative, I hope this visit isn't going to become a regular occurrence," he said testily. "It upsets my schedule."

Detective Inspector Richardson smiled. "I'm sure it won't," he said. "We have almost finished our investigation. We just have a few things to clear up."

Freemen relaxed back into his soft leather chair. "Good. In that case, how can I help you this morning, Detective?"

"Well," Richardson said, "this has been an interesting case. We started off with a short list of suspects and I have interviewed those most likely to have been involved. On the first day, I was offered three theories about what had happened to the Prometheus. Samuel Carter thought it had been sabotaged by the Chinese and Dr O'Connor, or Brother Columba as he now is, was sure that it would turn out to be a bizarre accident caused by the technical ineptness of Dr DeWitt. Dr Proctor, on the other hand, thought that Dr DeWitt was so upset that no one would believe his theories that he deliberately murdered his two companions, accidentally killing himself in the process."

"As I told you yesterday, all of these seem equally possible and equally implausible," Freeman said. "Which have you decided is the answer?"

"None of them," Richardson answered. "As you say, they are all implausible and none fit the circumstances of the Prometheus crew members' deaths." Richardson paused and seemed to be consulting his wrist data terminal. "You didn't offer any theory, Professor. Why is that?" he asked casually. Freeman remained silent. "I think it's because you knew precisely how they died. You knew that because it was you who killed them."

"What utter nonsense," the professor said sharply. "What do you base that on? You accuse me of murder just because I didn't offer some crackpot theory, a theory that could only have been based on wild speculation? Well, that's just crazy. Look, you really want a theory? Well, here's one. It was Mars. They were on an alien planet that we still don't understand and it was dangerous. Unexplained things happen and there are any number of ways in which electrical systems can be burnt out: a violent electrical storm or the sort of electro-magnetic pulse associated with volcanic action."

Detective Inspector Richardson seemed to consider the reply for a moment. When he replied it was with a tired and rather sad voice. "Unfortunately, Professor, there is no indication that such storms occur on Mars. You, an atmospheric physicist, should know this. Also, there was no volcanic activity recorded anywhere near the Hellas Basin at the time. There was, however, a substantial power outage recorded on the orbiter Ares II that can't be accounted for. I think it was caused by the MMS suddenly drawing a lot of power. At about the same time as this power use occurred, the recording of your instrument log was disabled for nearly five minutes. Long enough for you to reconfigure the MSS and send a microwave beam to the surface with sufficient power to destroy a spacecraft's electrical systems."

Freeman felt his heart go cold inside him. He'd been stupid. Still, there was one card he could still play, one secret he knew no one would tell. "That's ridiculous," he said. "Why would I do that? What motive could I possibly have? I pointed this out to you the other day. I have no motive to do such a thing. I'm good at what I do. I would have had a successful career no matter what."

The detective nodded, considering the questions. "Yes, but maybe not the one you wanted," he said. "I'll admit that motive was a real puzzle. There you were, a young astronaut who could expect to return to glory and adulation no matter what happened. Why would a delay of a few months be so important that you would kill your friends to avoid it?"

"Exactly," the professor said. "The whole notion is ridiculous."

"Not that ridiculous, actually," Richardson said. "When I thought about your current position as

Professor of Atmospheric Physics, I realised that you were primarily a scientist and an academic. For you, being an astronaut was mainly a way of gaining data, of increasing your academic standing. The praise of the popular press, while undoubtedly pleasant, would mean little to you. What did mean something to you was the praise of your peers, your professional colleagues. What you wanted was the prestige of being the author of the definitive book, the glory of making that fundamental discovery and carving out your own piece of scientific history. What do they call it? The Freeman Effect? Orographic microconvection in the Martian atmosphere – you discovered that, didn't you? It changed the way we think about Martian weather." Professor Freeman remained silent. "In the face of that, the academic power, position and even money that would go with all this was all just a happy bonus – the cherry on top. To achieve these aims, however, you had to kill that crew on the surface."

"Oh, and why was that?" the professor asked with scathing sarcasm. Even as he was talking, Detective Inspector Richardson was watching Freeman closely. Alarm bells were ringing in the back of the detective's mind. The man's body language was wrong, his reactions were off. Richardson's instincts told him that he was missing something important, something central to the case, but his mind couldn't isolate what it was. He continued with his explanation, trusting that any problems would sort themselves out in time.

"The Prometheus had suffered a propulsion failure and your ship had been ordered to stay in orbit and provide support until a relief ship could be organised," Richardson said. "Since the next mission, a Chinese effort, as it happened, was already well advanced, there was nothing terribly difficult or dangerous about this. It was an inconvenience, nothing more. It did, however, mean a delay of about eighteen months in your return to Earth."

"So what?" Freeman asked. "I already had my data."

"But that's the point, isn't it?" Richardson insisted. "You already had your data but so did everyone else. If your return was substantially delayed, your data would have been transmitted, in their entirety, to Earth. This would mean that, for a further eighteen months, you would have had to work with the limited computing available on board a spaceship while your rivals on Earth would've had far better facilities. They would've been able to interact with the world's best supercomputers, to work on the data that you collected. Of course, you would have some unique advantages, but the extra time gap could have been sufficient to make the difference between being *the* expert in the field and being *an* expert. You might even have been relegated from the position of the chief scientist of Martian atmospheric physics to that of the field hand: the man who collected the data that others analysed and interpreted. The Freeman Effect may have had a very different name." Richardson was worried. Freeman wasn't reacting properly. In fact, he wasn't reacting much at all. He was becoming more and more disengaged.

"So you killed the stranded surface crew, knowing that when their radio went silent and stayed silent your ship would be allowed to return home," he continued. "It's all a bit more complicated than I would like but I think a jury will accept it."

"Really?" Freeman asked. "Will they really believe that I am a person so cold, so devoid of feeling that I would kill for the contents of a scientific paper?"

Richardson shrugged. "They might, they might not," he said. "But they will certainly know that a delayed return would have worked against you professionally. They will know that you benefitted from the deaths of the crew on the surface and that you knew you would at the time. No one doubts that you are talented but your publication record clearly shows that your career is built on the wreckage of the Prometheus." Richardson noted that Freeman didn't react with outrage or anger. He wasn't even afraid. He seemed to have relaxed into a sort of detachment.

"This is all supposition," he said in a flat, calm voice. "You have no proof, and," he added softly, "you don't understand anything. You are quite wrong."

Detective Inspector Richardson also answered calmly. "Well, now, Professor, you had motive and that microwave sounding equipment made you one of only three people who had any real opportunity. Then there is the business of the power use and the disabled instrument log. There is something else also. When I came into this room there were only eight people who knew that the Prometheus crew had suffocated because a total electronics failure had caused the breakdown of their life support systems. The four expedition members who found the wreck and carried out the preliminary investigation knew. They sent a special coded message to the director of the United Nations Space Agency who personally briefed me. I personally briefed Detective Sergeant Wilson here. Besides the seven of us, the only other person who could know was the murderer. You, Professor Freeman, didn't offer a weird theory for the deaths because you knew how they had died. You knew of the electronics failure. Professor Freeman, I arrest you for the murders of Doctors Cole and DeWitt and Colonel Prentice. You have the right to remain silent …"

Memory is a strange and wonderful thing. In his mind's eye Freeman could still see her as she was when they had first met, with her blonde hair tied up to fit beneath her flight helmet: a pilot first, second and third. He didn't remember the other two that clearly. Still, it was the three of them together who condemned him by their death. Suddenly, he knew the answer to his question. It had not been worth it. The price was too high. This was going to cost him everything. He felt something break deep inside his soul.

"No!" he yelled. He stood up suddenly, as if catapulted from his seat by the force of his exclamation. Richardson stopped giving him his rights and looked at him in surprise. Sergeant Wilson moved to block the door.

Professor Freeman stood behind his desk shaking. Darkness began to close around the periphery of his vision. Then ... then he knew what he had to do. Only three more steps and he would be free.

It was spring and the elm trees that dotted the campus were a vivid green. Behind him the bulk of Detective Inspector Richardson moved with surprising speed, but too late. The morning sun was brilliant and it reflected brightly from the broken shards of glass as they fell to the ground. He was weightless again, as he had been twenty years ago, dreaming a nightmare behind his instrument panel. With a sharp crack the darkness closed completely on his mind.

Chapter Fourteen – Aftermath

As Mars approached solar periapsis, its closest approach to the sun, the southern hemisphere started to heat up and the frozen carbon dioxide covering the southern ice cap began to evaporate. On the floor of the Hellas Basin, the wind rose. Dust blew and sand shifted. The sky darkened with the storm. Soon all the track marks and footprints were obliterated and all was as it had been before. Only the bodies were missing, taken away to be marked and remembered by their own kind.

It was late in the day and the forensics team were finishing up their work. Chief Inspector Roger Gordon was happily briefing the press on the outcome of the investigation, heaping praise on Richardson but basking in the glory himself. Richardson didn't care. He was just glad, very glad, he didn't have to talk to the press himself. Nevertheless, he was frowning as he finally got into the car and asked Wilson to drive him home.

"What's wrong, boss?" Wilson asked. "You should be happy. This is a real feather in your cap. You just solved the ultimate cold case, murders that happened twenty years ago and on another planet, and you did it in just under three days. This is the stuff of legend." Richardson just grunted, clearly unhappy. Wilson considered his boss's mood as he pulled out into the traffic.

"You think you got the wrong man?" he asked.

Richardson shook his head. "No, I'm sure he was guilty," he answered. "It's just that something has bothered me about this case right from the beginning. It's just been too easy. It ran almost like a scripted play. Also, Freeman's reactions and body language were always weird. Why? Because he already knew that we would be coming for him. He knew that we would find him out."

Wilson shrugged. "Well, he was guilty, wasn't he?" he said. "You know, the guilty flee … etc."

"It's not only that," Richardson said. "They asked for me by name. Why? Because they knew that I was good, that I could be depended on to follow the trail of breadcrumbs and get the right answer. But they also knew that I, a local policeman, wouldn't have the resources to look much beyond that trail. I was led to find Freeman guilty by someone who already knew that he was. The question is, how did they know? I hate loose ends, especially important ones, and I don't like being treated like a puppet, a mere functionary."

Wilson smiled; being treated like a mere functionary was something he was used to. "Just relax and enjoy it, boss," he said. Richardson sat back and scowled at the Melbourne traffic. Then he pulled out a small tablet and started reviewing the case files. All the data were the same as they had been before; there was nothing beyond the trail of breadcrumbs he now believed he had been manipulated into following. In disgust, he handed the tablet to Wilson as they pulled up outside his house. Wilson flipped through a few screens while Richardson gathered up his things. He stopped at a picture of the mission commander and Colonel Prentice sitting at an outdoor table.

"When and where was this photo taken, boss?" he asked.

"It was in Alice Springs," Richardson answered after glancing casually at the photo. "A passing tourist recognised the commander and put the photo up on their social media page. From their expressions, they weren't too happy about being photographed. Don't blame them, fame can be a pest."

"So, you didn't look at it too closely," Wilson said.

"No," Richardson replied. He took the tablet back, curious about what his sergeant was getting at. "I checked out the timing. It was just after one of the initial mission training exercises at Gosse's Bluff. It's only in the file because the computer highlighted the names. I discounted it. After all, it's only two crew members having lunch together after a training exercise. Surely they're allowed to do that."

"Boss, you're getting old," Wilson said smiling. "Left hand … finger … both of them."

Richardson looked at the image and suddenly its significance dawned on him. Everything – the priority given to the investigation, the incredible security, the motive for murder – it all slotted neatly into place and he knew he'd been used.

"Shit," he said. "Shit, shit, shit …"

Chapter Fifteen – Motive

Half a world away, in a plush and expensive office that befitted the status of its occupant, William Chang sat alone well after office hours: Dr William Chang, formerly commander of the Ares II mission to the planet Mars and currently Director of the United Nations Space Agency, one of the most powerful people on Earth. Against one wall there was an archaic bookshelf filled with antique, hardcover volumes. In stark contrast, the opposite wall was dominated by a holographic image of the surface of Mars. It showed a space-suited astronaut giving a mock military salute to the United Nations Flag. Behind him stretched the monotonous plain and endless red dust that formed the floor of the Hellas Basin. A third wall was a ceiling-to-floor window which showed a confusion of lights as the city of Geneva worked through the night.

Dr Chang had a glass in his hand and there was a half-empty bottle of whiskey on his desk. On his finger was a ring that he hadn't worn for twenty years. He was looking at a photograph which he normally kept locked in his private desk drawer. It was the photograph of a young woman in her early thirties, dressed in a green flight suit. She was blonde and attractive in a competent, 'no nonsense' sort of way. Dr Chang shook his head with sorrow. After all these years he must still keep their secret. Only one other person had ever found out and that had caused total disaster. They had tried to warn him off but how could they have known what his reaction would be?

He ground his teeth in both anger and grief, undiminished by the years.

"I got him for you, Elise," he said, his voice slurred by drink and emotion. "It's only now I could do it. It's taken me years but I made him pay. Just like I swore he would." His eyes filled with tears as he raised his glass in one more toast to the memory of his wife.

Epilogue

After the funeral, Father Mulcahey was glad to relax in the quarters assigned to him at Schiparelli Base. It had been a busy day. The funeral of the three long-dead explorers had been a huge and formal affair, full of officials from the agency and base management. He needed to rest. Tomorrow he had two baptisms and a wedding, as well as the routine duties of a visiting chaplain. Yet he found it hard to settle into his prayers and kept looking out his window to the reddish hills of the crater rim.

It was a sad and yet somehow appropriate thing, he thought, to be mourning death on a dead planet, a planet where life just never took hold. Then he corrected himself. No, this was a planet where life is only now starting to take hold. He thought of the couple he would marry tomorrow, finally free of the restrictions of the agency and setting out on their own. He thought of the children he would baptise, of the people of the base who did not work for the space agency, getting married and raising families. Earth was losing control. Life is just beginning on this planet, he thought, and in the final analysis, that's why we're here. He smiled then, as he settled into his meditations.

Dear Reader,

Thank you for reading my book. If you enjoyed it, please take a moment to review the work at your favourite retailer. Also, if you enjoy cross-over murder mysteries, you might enjoy *The Answerer,* a fantasy murder mystery in the mythical land a Tyr Na nOg. It involves kidnapping, a magical kingdom, five murders, and the theft of a magical sword of legendary power. Young Irish policeman, Sean MacCarthy, certainly has a very interesting day. Available at all good e-book retailers.

Thank you,

Joseph H.J. Liaigh